written by
KiRSTY APPLEBAUM

SAHAR HAGHGOO

PRiNCESS MiNNA

THE BEST PRINCESS

nosy crow

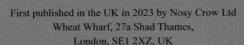

First published in the UK in 2023 by Nosy Crow Ltd
Wheat Wharf, 27a Shad Thames,
London, SE1 2XZ, UK

Nosy Crow Eireann Ltd
44 Orchard Grove, Kenmare,
Co Kerry, V93 FY22, Ireland

Nosy Crow and associated logos are trademarks and/or registered
trademarks of Nosy Crow Ltd.

ISBN: 978 1 83994 802 2

A CIP catalogue record for this book will be available from the British Library.

Printed and bound in Poland.

Papers used by Nosy Crow are made from wood grown in sustainable forests.

1 3 5 7 9 10 8 6 4 2

www.nosycrow.com

MIX
Paper | Supporting
responsible forestry
FSC® C018236

PRINCESS MINNA

THE BEST PRINCESS

More **ROYALLY EXCITING ADVENTURES** to look out for:

PRINCESS MINNA

THE ENCHANTED FOREST

THE UNICORN MIX-UP

THE BIG BAD SNOWY DAY

THE WICKED WOOD

Chapter One

This is Minna. She is a **princess**.

Princess Minna is very good at **lots** of things.

She is good at taming unicorns, kissing frogs and fighting dragons.

1

Princess Minna has a magic mirror. It hangs on her bedroom wall. Sometimes she stands in front of it and says, "Mirror, mirror, on the wall, who's the best princess of all?"

The mirror always makes the same reply. "Why, **you** of course, Princess Minna. You are the best princess in all the kingdom."

Princess Minna
thinks the magic
mirror is **great.**

3

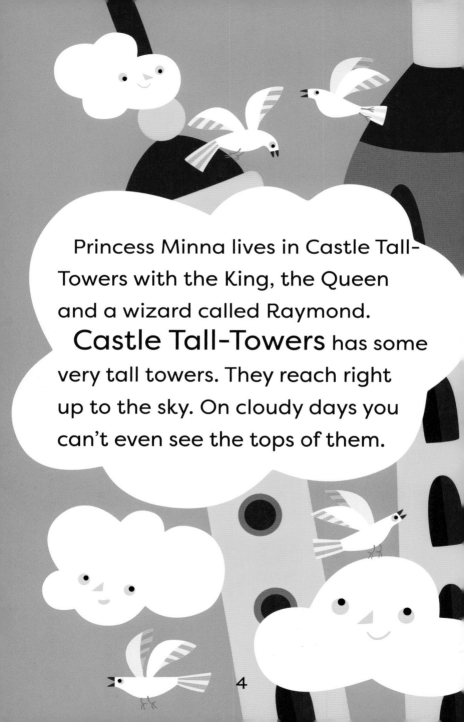

Princess Minna lives in Castle Tall-Towers with the King, the Queen and a wizard called Raymond.
Castle Tall-Towers has some very tall towers. They reach right up to the sky. On cloudy days you can't even see the tops of them.

4

When all is well in the kingdom, lots of grey doves **sweep** and **swoop** around the towers making soft cooing noises. They make the whole castle smell like **tutti-frutti** ice cream.

When all is **not** well in the kingdom,

big

seagulls fly up from the coast and scare the doves away.

Then they

flip and flap

around the towers, making
screechy, **squawking** noises.
They make the whole castle smell
like old seaweed.

One morning, Princess Minna remembered that she hadn't spoken to her magic mirror for a few days. She had been **too busy** making a Tyrannosaurus rex out of milk-bottle tops. She wanted to make a Stegosaurus too, but there weren't any milk-bottle tops left.

She got out of bed and went straight to her magic mirror.

She smiled at it and said:

glue

"Mirror, mirror, on the wall, who's the best princess of all?"

9

"Umm..." replied the mirror.

That's strange, thought Princess Minna. The mirror doesn't usually say **umm**.

She tried again.

"Mirror, mirror, on the wall, who's the best princess of all?"

"Umm..." said the mirror.

Goodness, thought Princess Minna. That is

very strange indeed.

She stopped.
She sniffed.
Was that the smell of ...
seaweed?

Flip!

Flap!

Screech!

Squawk!

A big seagull flew past her window.

Oh dear. All was **not** well in the kingdom.

13

"Your Most Royal Highness," said the mirror, "I have to tell the whole truth at all times."

"Of course," said Princess Minna. "We must all tell the truth."

"Well," said the mirror, "at the moment,

Princess Sky-Blue

is the best princess in all the kingdom."

"Princess Sky-Blue?" cried
Princess Minna.
"I'm afraid so, Your Most Royal
Highness."

15

"But Princess Sky-Blue lives in a neighbouring kingdom. It doesn't count!"

"That is true," said the mirror, "but she's taking a little holiday and right now she is in **this** kingdom."

A new face slowly appeared in the magic glass. A face with

a smile as wide as the sky

and

hair as blue as sapphire.

It was Princess Sky-Blue.

"Oh dear," said Princess Minna. "Oh dear, oh dear, oh dear." She ran all the way downstairs.

"Minna!" said the Queen. "Thank goodness you're here. There are seagulls **everywhere**."

"All is not well in the kingdom," said the King.

19

"I know," said Princess Minna.
"It's because Princess Sky-Blue
is here. I'm not the best princess
any more." She sat down at the
table feeling rather sad.

"Oh," said the Queen. "Could
you sort it out, please, Minna?

20

There are seagull feathers in our breakfast."

"Yes," agreed the King, "and please hurry up or there'll be feathers in our elevenses as well..."

"...and then where will we be?" said the Queen.

They're right, thought Princess Minna. I must sort this out. I must make sure that Princess Sky-Blue **leaves** the kingdom

once and for all.

Then the doves will come back to Castle Tall-Towers and I will be the **best princess** again. She gulped down her breakfast and ran out of the castle.

23

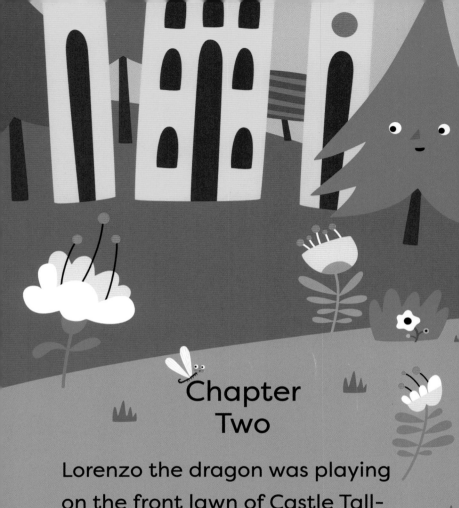

Chapter Two

Lorenzo the dragon was playing on the front lawn of Castle Tall-Towers. He was Princess Minna's best friend in the whole world.

Princess Minna climbed on to his back. "Can you take me into town, please?" she said. "Princess Sky-Blue is here and I need to find her **urgently**."

Lorenzo flapped his great wings and swished his great tail and the two of them flew up, up, up into the sky.

Wallooop wallooop wallooop!

When they
reached the town,
Princess Minna
was confused.
The townspeople
had already done
all the things they
do when a princess
comes to visit.

28

They had already
put up the bunting
... they had already baked
sponge cakes with cream in
the middle ... and they had
already brought their babies
out to be kissed.

29

"How did you know I was
coming?" said Princess Minna.
"Even I didn't know I was coming."

"Oh, these aren't for you," said
the townspeople. "These are for
Princess Sky-Blue. Have you met
her? She's lovely."

"Her smile is as wide as the sky!"

"Her hair is as blue as sapphire!"

"She bought toast in our shop," said Little Tommy Turret from Turret's T shop.

"She bought biscuits in our shop," said Little Betty Button from Button's B shop.

"She bought a huge jar of pickled pineapple in ours," said Little Pippi Piper from Piper's P shop.

Princess Minna frowned. She looked at the bunting. She looked at the sponge cakes. She looked at the babies. She crossed her angry arms.

"Where is Princess Sky-Blue now?" she said.

"She's in the park, eating her pickled pineapple," said Little Pippi.

Just at that moment, a cheerful milkmaid walked past. She was wearing a white apron and a pretty bonnet.

This gave Princess Minna a

brilliant idea.

"Excuse me," she said. "Please may I borrow your white apron and your pretty bonnet?"

"Of course," said the cheerful milkmaid.

Princess Minna put on the apron and the bonnet, then ran all the way to the park.

There was Princess
Sky-Blue, eating her pickled
pineapple.

Princess Minna was now
cleverly disguised as a cheerful
milkmaid. She grabbed the
pickled pineapple from
Princess Sky-Blue.

36

"Oh don't eat that, I beg you!" cried Princess Minna. "All the pickled pineapple in our kingdom has been poisoned. Everyone is SO sick. You must leave the kingdom immediately and go home to your mum."

In truth, the pickled pineapple wasn't poisoned at all, but Princess Sky-Blue wasn't to know.

"**Crikey**," Princess Sky-Blue said. "That's

terribly bad news.

But don't worry. One of my special skills is **mixing marvellous medicines**."

Before Princess Minna could stop her, Princess Sky-Blue had mixed up a magical cure.

She sprinkled the cure over
Princess Minna. Then she ran
around town sprinkling everyone
else, too.

41

Then she gathered up all the
pickled pineapple she could find
and threw it in the bin.

Gosh, thought Princess Minna.
Princess Sky-Blue is really quite
good at sorting things out.

She crossed her angry arms again. She needed to come up with a **better plan**. Princess Sky-Blue **must** leave the kingdom once and for all, or she would **always** be the best princess.

Chapter
Three

A little bit later, Princess Minna
went back to the townspeople.
"Where is Princess Sky-Blue
now?" she asked.

"She's on the bench, eating her biscuits," said Little Betty Button from Button's B shop.

Just at that moment, a well-to-do gentleman walked past. He was wearing a top hat and walking with a cane.

This gave Princess Minna another

brilliant idea.

This one was

much more brilliant

than the first.

"Excuse me," she said. "Please may I borrow your top hat and your walking cane?"

"Of course," said the well-to-do gentleman.

Princess Minna put on the hat, gave the cane a quick twirl, then ran all the way to the bench.

There was Princess Sky-Blue,
eating her biscuits.

Princess Minna was now
cleverly disguised as a well-to-do
gentleman. She shooed Princess
Sky-Blue away from the bench.

"Oh, don't sit there, I beg you!"
cried Princess Minna. "An evil
monster lurks in a mysterious cave
over there. It snatches one person
away every day! Soon we will

all be gone.

You must leave the kingdom
immediately and go home to your
mum."

In truth, there was no evil monster
lurking in the mysterious cave, but
Princess Sky-Blue wasn't to know.

"Jeepers," said Princess Sky-Blue. "That is **stonkingly bad news**. But don't worry. One of my special skills is **guessing the passwords to mysterious caves.**

I can guess the cave's password, close the entrance and lock your evil monster in **forever**."

Before Princess Minna could stop her, Princess Sky-Blue had inspected the outside of the cave and done lots of tricky sums in her notepad.

Then she took a deep breath and chanted some strange magical words.

"Vlimmery vlammery zlimmery zlammery!"

A large stone slid across the front of the mysterious cave, sealing it up for all eternity.

"All fixed," said Princess Sky-Blue. "That evil monster won't be giving you any more trouble."

Princess Minna crossed her angry arms again. Princess Sky-Blue was very good at being a princess. She **really must** leave the kingdom once and for all.

55

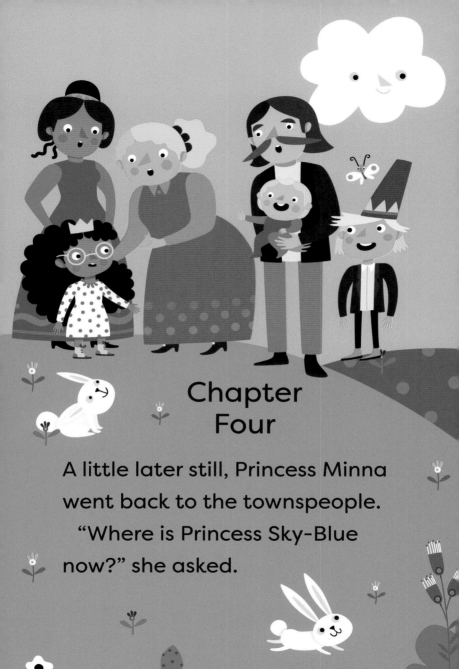

Chapter
Four

A little later still, Princess Minna
went back to the townspeople.
"Where is Princess Sky-Blue
now?" she asked.

"She's under that tree, eating her toast," said Little Tommy Turret from Turret's T shop.

Just at that moment, a fearless police constable walked past. She was wearing her police-constable hat and eating an ice cream.

This gave Princess Minna yet another

brilliant idea.

This one was

even more brilliant

than the other two.

"Excuse me," she said. "Please
may I borrow your police-constable
hat and your ice cream?"

"Of course," said the fearless
police constable.

Princess Minna put on the hat.
Then she turned the ice cream
upside down and stuck it on
Lorenzo's head. After that, she
ran all the way to the tree.

There was Princess Sky-Blue, eating her toast.

Princess Minna was now cleverly disguised as a fearless police constable. She pulled Princess Sky-Blue up from the ground.

"Oh, don't stay there, I beg you!" cried Princess Minna. "There's a wild unicorn gallivanting about!"

Sure enough, there was a wild unicorn. It had big wings and a long, blue, dragony tail.

In truth, it wasn't really a wild unicorn at all. It was Lorenzo with an ice-cream cone on his head. But Princess Sky-Blue wasn't to know.

Princess Sky-Blue looked carefully at Lorenzo. There was ice cream dripping down his face.

"Are you sure that's a unicorn?" she said.

"Yes!" said Princess Minna. "It's **incredibly** dangerous. You must leave the kingdom immediately and go home to your mum."

But just at that moment, a

real

wild unicorn gallivanted past.
It began to cause mayhem
all over town.

65

"We have a

unicorn
emergency!"

cried the townspeople.
"Where is Princess Minna?"
Princess Minna didn't know
what to do.

Should she carry on pretending to
be a fearless police constable
until Princess Sky-Blue had left
the kingdom? Or should she reveal
her true identity and tame the
unicorn?

She watched as the unicorn
pulled down all the pretty bunting.

Then she watched as the unicorn
ate up all the delicious sponge
cake.

"Where are you, Princess Minna?"
called the townspeople. "We need
your help!"

Next, the unicorn started to scare
the babies.

Princess Minna couldn't watch
any longer.

She had to tame the unicorn, even if it meant Princess Sky-Blue **never** left the kingdom and was **always** the best princess.

"Don't worry," shouted Princess Minna. "I'm here!" She took off her clever disguise.

70

"Hurrah!" called
the townspeople.

71

Princess Minna chased after the real wild unicorn. She **stroked and whispered** and **whispered and stroked** until it became happy and calm. It trotted away, leaving the town in peace.

Chapter
Five

"**Wowzers**," said Princess Sky-Blue. "You're not really a fearless police constable at all."

"No," said Princess Minna. "I'm Princess Minna. My magic mirror used to tell me that I was the best princess. But ever since you came to the kingdom, it says **you're** the best princess. I've been trying to make you leave so that I can be the best again."

75

"**Princess Minna**!" Princess Sky-Blue's eyes grew as wide as her smile. "This is **so cool**. I've always wanted to meet you."

"You have?" said Princess Minna.

"Yes! Your unicorn-taming is famous throughout the land. Will you show me how to do it?"

Princess Minna and Princess Sky-Blue spent a very happy afternoon together. Princess Minna showed Princess Sky-Blue how to kiss frogs,

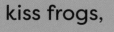

76

tame unicorns

and fight dragons.

Princess Sky-Blue showed Princess Minna how to mix marvellous medicines and guess the passwords to mysterious caves.

She also showed her how to spin straw into precious things, because that was her other special skill.

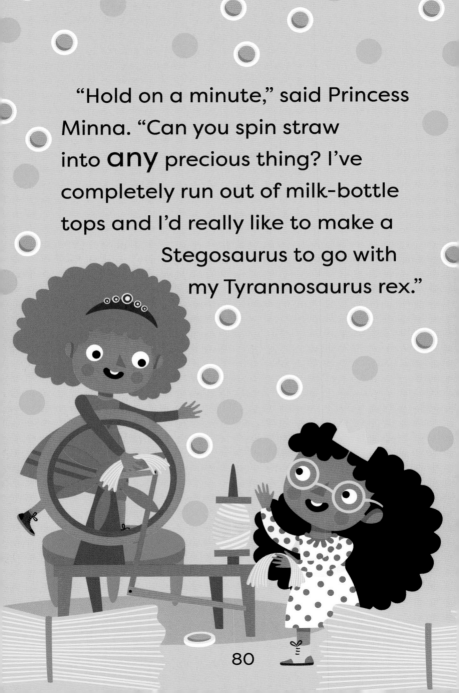

"Hold on a minute," said Princess Minna. "Can you spin straw into **any** precious thing? I've completely run out of milk-bottle tops and I'd really like to make a Stegosaurus to go with my Tyrannosaurus rex."

"Easy-peasy!" said Princess Sky-Blue.

The two princesses spent the next few days together, spinning straw into milk-bottle tops and building the **best Stegosaurus ever.**

"I have to go home tonight," said Princess Sky-Blue as they put the final milk-bottle top into place. "My mum is expecting me back."

"I'm sorry I tried to scare you away from the kingdom," said Princess Minna. "I'm

very

glad it didn't work. I'm never going to ask my magic mirror about the best princess again."

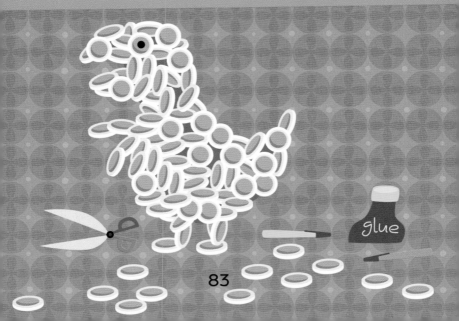

"Good idea," said Princess Sky-Blue. "I've got eleven older sisters, so my mirror always thinks **someone** is a better princess than me. It's not true, though.

We're just different, that's all."

"But," she added, "there is **one** good thing about magic mirrors. We can use them to keep in touch with each other!"

Later that evening Princess Minna stood in front of her magic mirror again. But this time she said:

"Mirror, mirror, on the wall, please give Princess Sky-Blue a call."

A face slowly appeared in the magic glass. It had **a smile as wide as the sky** and **hair as blue as sapphire**.

"Hello, Princess Sky-Blue!" said Princess Minna.

"Hello, Princess Minna!" said
Princess Sky-Blue.

The two princesses talked about unicorns and dragons and mysterious caves until bedtime.

89

Doves cooed outside the window
and the whole castle smelled of
tutti-frutti ice cream.
And **all was well** in the
kingdom once more.